Dear Parent:
Your child's love of reading starts here!

Every child learns to read in a different way and at his or her own speed. Some go back and forth between reading levels and read favorite books again and again. Others read through each level in order. You can help your young reader improve and become more confident by encouraging his or her own interests and abilities. From books your child reads with you to the first books he or she reads alone, there are I Can Read Books for every stage of reading:

SHARED READING
Basic language, word repetition, and whimsical illustrations, ideal for sharing with your emergent reader

BEGINNING READING
Short sentences, familiar words, and simple concepts for children eager to read on their own

READING WITH HELP
Engaging stories, longer sentences, and language play for developing readers

READING ALONE
Complex plots, challenging vocabulary, and high-interest topics for the independent reader

ADVANCED READING
Short paragraphs, chapters, and exciting themes for the perfect bridge to chapter books

I Can Read Books have introduced children to the joy of reading since 1957. Featuring award-winning authors and illustrators and a fabulous cast of beloved characters, I Can Read Books set the standard for beginning readers.

A lifetime of discovery begins with the magical words "I Can Read!"

Visit www.icanread.com for information
on enriching your child's reading experience.

For Tamar and her wonderful,
pearly white smile!
—J.O'C.

For Alex,
whose smile lights up a room!
—R.P.G.

For P.S., who (I think)
bought me my first-ever set
of plastic Dracula fangs
—T.E.

I Can Read Book® is a trademark of HarperCollins Publishers.

Fancy Nancy and the Too-Loose Tooth Text copyright © 2012 by Jane O'Connor Illustrations copyright © 2012 by Robin Preiss Glasser All rights reserved. Manufactured in China. No part of this book may be used or reproduced in any manner whatsoever without written permission except in the case of brief quotations embodied in critical articles and reviews. For information address HarperCollins Children's Books, a division of HarperCollins Publishers, 10 East 53rd Street, New York, NY 10022. www.icanread.com

Library of Congress Cataloging-in-Publication Data is available.
ISBN 978-0-06-208301-2 (trade bdg.) — ISBN 978-0-06-208302-9 (pbk.)

12 13 14 15 16 SCP 10 9 8 7 6 5 4 3 2 1 ❖ First Edition

Fancy NANCY and the Too-Loose Tooth

by Jane O'Connor

cover illustration by Robin Preiss Glasser

interior illustrations by Ted Enik

HARPER

An Imprint of HarperCollinsPublishers

Lionel and I are swinging
on the monkey bars.
Lionel swings upside down.

"Whoo! Whoo! I am an ape!"

Lionel shouts, and

scratches under his arms.

Lionel swings again.

He bangs into a bar.

"Ow!" he says.

Lionel jumps to the ground.

I jump down too.

His hand is over his mouth.

There is a little gore!

(Gore is a fancy word for blood.)

"Come quick, Ms. Glass!"

I shout.

"Lionel is injured."

(That's fancy for hurt.)

"I am okay."

Lionel smiles.

He lost a tooth!

It is in his hand.

"It was already loose."

10

Ms. Glass lets me go

to the nurse with Lionel.

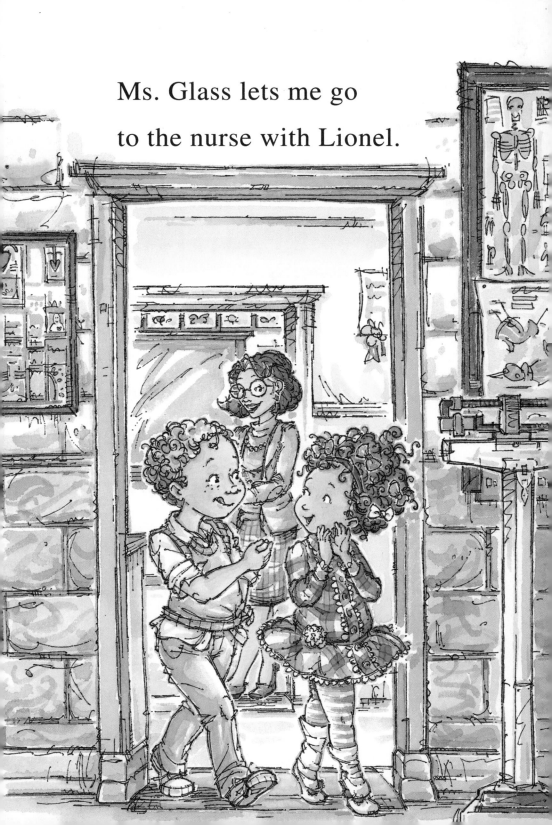

First Lionel washes out his mouth.

Ms. Glass lets me go
to the nurse with Lionel.

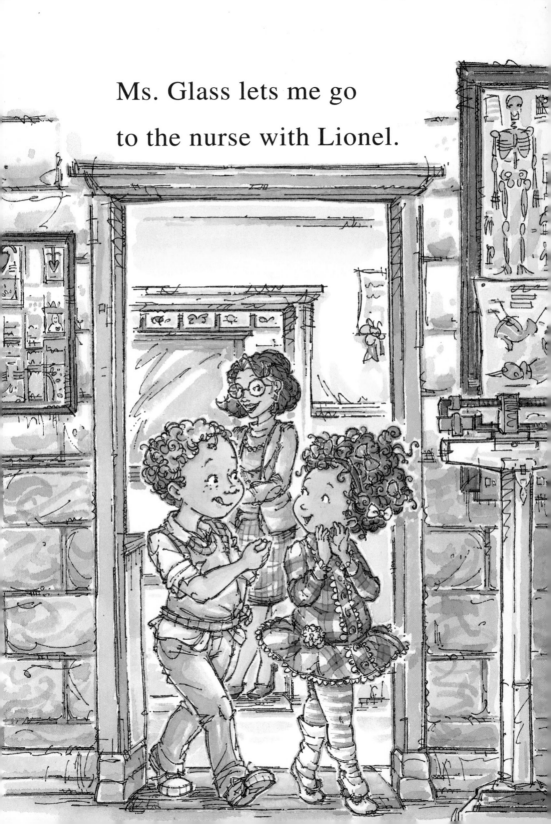

First Lionel washes out his mouth.

Then the nurse hands Lionel

a white plastic tooth on a chain.

Pop! The top opens.

In goes the tooth.

Pop! The top snaps shut.

13

For the rest of the day,

Lionel wears his tooth necklace.

I long for a tooth necklace too.

(That means I really, really

want one.)

But you only get one if

your tooth falls out at school.

One of my teeth is loose now.

It better not fall out at home!

All week my tooth
gets looser and looser.
I wiggle it a lot at school.
I wiggle it in art class.
I wiggle it at lunch.

At home I do not wiggle it at all.

I eat a lot of soft stuff, like

bananas and ice cream.

I don't talk much.

Talking might make

my tooth fall out.

My dad asks,

"Want me to pull out your tooth?

It won't hurt."

"No!" I shout.

It can't fall out at home!

On Thursday at school,

my tooth is hanging by a thread.

I keep waiting for it to fall out.

But the last bell rings and

my tooth is still stuck in my head.

I must prevent my tooth

from falling out tonight!

(Prevent means to stop something.)

I put a little tape around it.

"What's wrong with your mouth?"
my mother asks.
I write a note to explain.
My tooth is very loose.
I don't want it to fall out
until I'm at school.
Then I'll get a tooth necklace.

That night,

I sleep with my mouth open.

I am not taking any chances.

Friday morning,

I get dressed very carefully.

I start walking to school.

"Achoo!" I sneeze.

Oh no!

Sneezing made my tooth fall out.

It's in my mouth!

I am not at school yet.

So does this mean

I don't deserve a tooth necklace?

But my tooth is still in my mouth.

So, in a way, it has not

fallen out yet.

I keep my lips shut tight.

I walk very fast.

At last I arrive at school.

(Arrive is fancy for

getting someplace.)

I spit my tooth into my hand.

"I just lost a tooth!" I shout.

Ms. Glass sends me to the nurse.

Ooh la la! I have a tooth necklace.

It looks so fancy.

I wear it all day.

But guess what?

I do not feel joyful.

(That's fancy for happy.)

Finally I confess.

Confess means telling

about something bad you did.

I tell Ms. Glass

how my tooth fell out.

"I need to return

the tooth necklace."

Ms. Glass thinks for a moment.

(A moment is fancy for a second.)

"Your tooth didn't fall out at home.

You were already in transit.

That means on the way to school.

I think that counts."

Ms. Glass checks with the nurse.

The nurse agrees.

The tooth necklace is mine
to keep forever!

For the first time all day,

I smile a big smile—

with a hole in it!

Fancy Nancy's Fancy Words

These are the fancy words in this book:

Arrive—getting someplace

Confess—telling about something bad you did

Gore—blood

Injured—hurt

In transit—on the way

Joyful—happy

Long for—really, really want

Moment—a second

Prevent—stop something